MASTER THOMAS KATT

Based on a Danish Folk-tale

Susan Price

Illustrated by Kate Simpson

A & C Black · London

The Comets Series

King Fernando	John Bartholomew
The Dream Seller	Terry Deary
A Witch in Time	Terry Deary
The Double	Heather Eyles
The Spaceball	Maggie Freeman
The Reversible Giant	Robert Leeson
Tom's Sausage Lion	Michael Morpurgo
Odin's Monster	Susan Price
Master Thomas Katt	Susan Price
Where Dragons Breathe	Jean Simister
Scrapyard	Andy Soutter
The Air-Raid Shelter	Jeremy Strong
Dogs are Different	Jeremy Strong
Liar, Liar, Pants on Fire!	Jeremy Strong
The Haunting Music	Robina Beckles Willson
Christina's Ghost	Betty Ren Wright

First published 1988 by A & C Black (Publishers) Ltd.,
35 Bedford Row, London WC1R 4JH

Text copyright © 1988 Susan Price
Illustrations copyright © 1988 Kate Simpson

British Library Cataloguing in Publication Data

Price, Susan, 1955–
  Master Thomas Katt.—(The Comets series).
  I. Title II. Simpson, Kate III. Series
  823'.914 [J]

ISBN 0-7136-3036-1

Filmset by August Filmsetting, Haydock, St Helens.
Printed in Great Britain by The Bath Press, Bath.

Master Thomas Kitten

All that I'm going to tell of, happened a long time ago, hundreds of years ago, before there were cars or electric lights, or gas-fires, or clean water running out of taps inside houses.

It all starts with an old woman and her husband. They'd been married for thirty-five years, and between them they kept a small farm. They weren't so old that they couldn't work, and they lived comfortably enough on their own vegetables and fruit, eggs from their chickens and milk from their cow. But they didn't have any children, even though they'd been married so long, and that bothered them. It made them sad and jealous to see much younger people with troops of children, when they had not a one. It didn't seem fair.

'I had this farm from my father,' the old man often said, 'and he had it from his father. It seems a shame that it'll go to a stranger once we're dead, old woman.'

'What can't be cured must be endured,' she would say angrily. 'So don't talk of it.'

Now the farm buildings were full of cats, wild ones and half-wild ones, of all the colours and patterns possible to cats. They lived by hunting, and would catch and eat rats, mice, birds, and even rabbits. They would steal, too, given a chance, so the old woman always had to be careful to close the kitchen door against them. But every so often, as a reward for keeping down the rats and mice, the old woman would put out a bowl of milk for them in the yard. Apart from that, the old couple didn't take any notice of the cats. They had too many other things to think about to care about cats.

But one little cat, a little ginger, tabby cat, began waiting for the old woman, at the spot where she usually put down a dish of milk.

'Oh, you think you're going to get milk, don't you? – but you're not!' she said to it, and stooped and scratched the top of its head. It lifted itself up on its back legs and pushed its hard little head against her fingers. When the old woman straightened and walked away, it jumped at her flapping skirt and caught its claws in the cloth. Feeling the tug, the old woman looked round. 'Oh, you little devil, you. Shoo, go on, shoo!'

The little cat ran away, but it came back every day, to see if milk had been put out. 'There's a clever little cat,' said the old woman to the old man. 'He knows I'm going to put milk down one day, and he'll be first to the dish when I do.' And, because the little ginger cat kept reminding her, the old woman put out milk more often; and then she began to put down one little saucer of milk whenever the ginger

4

cat came, just enough for him to drink. The little cat began to know her, and to lean against her and purr when she came into the yard; and the old woman began to look out for him, and to call him to her, and to give him little treats – a scrap of cheese, a little bit of bacon-fat, a fish-skin; a lump of dripping which he would lick from her finger with a warm, rasping tongue. She liked him because he seemed to like her; that was the way of it.

Thomas, the old woman called him, because he was a little tom-cat. One day, when the old woman was slow in closing her kitchen door, Thomas skipped in behind her. She would have driven any other cat out, but she let Thomas stay, and watched him as she worked. It was amusing to see him running about the floor, looking into everything with a cat's curiosity. He jumped into chairs and on to the dresser; poked his little head into cupboards, and walked along the mantlepiece without knocking down a single ornament. Then he came to her and reached his front paws up to her with pleading mews.

'What do you want – milk? Milk, is it?' And the little cat was so pretty that she fetched a small saucer and poured a drop into it. Thomas scurried to it with his tail straight in the air and began to lap and purr at the same time. 'Wasting good milk on the likes of you,' the old woman said to him. 'Don't you tell the old man, will you?'

The old man didn't like the cat being in the house at first, because cats had never been allowed into the house before. But he saw that it made his wife happy to have the cat about, so he said nothing. And when Thomas jumped on to his knee one night, he felt pleased to be chosen to be sat on, and it was pleasant to stroke the little cat's soft fur and hear it grumble happily to itself. Soon Thomas came into the house whenever he liked; one of the old couple would even get up in the evening to let him in if he mewed outside. 'Come and sit on Mummy's knee,' the old woman would say to him, patting her knee, and she was delighted and proud if he ran across the floor and jumped on her lap.

'Shall I plant potatoes in topfield, or turnips, Tommy?' the old man would ask him, and the old woman would say, 'Oh, my feet are tired. Why don't you run and put the kettle on for me, Tommy?'

And though Tommy never answered, or put the kettle on, the old couple didn't mind. 'Oh you, you don't want to work, you only want to play,' the old woman said to him, and took a cotton reel from her sewing box and, as she sat in her chair, dragged it about on a thread of cotton, for Tommy to chase. He would crouch low, his bottom waggling; and then spring into the air and come down, biting, on the cotton-reel. Or he would bounce away from it, sideways, his four legs all stiff under him and his

back arched. Just watching him made the old
couple laugh until their eyes watered. And you
grow fond of anyone who makes you laugh.

It gave the old couple pleasure just to see their
little Tommy, grown plump and sleek, lying flat in
front of the fire with his cattish, contented smile. It
gave them pleasure to let him into their house out of
the rain, and to put dishes of milk and broth before
him, or a cracked egg. 'There you are, my lover,'
the old woman would croon. 'You enjoy it, you
gobble it all down and grow up big and strong.'

And though the old man pretended not to care
for the cat as much as his wife did, he would slip
Tommy bits of bacon from his plate, and call him

on to his lap, and stroke him, and no longer even thought of throwing him outside.

One evening the old woman said to her husband, 'Our little Tommy's growing up fast, old man; we should think of his future.'

'He'll have the farm,' said the old man. 'It's a good little farm.'

'But just think, if he had some education, he could be a better farmer than his old man,' said the old woman. 'He could keep his accounts better; he could read books and learn new things. We should do our best for him.'

'Well . . .' said the old man.

'After all, we don't need him on the farm yet; we can still manage on our own for a good few more years. We should let him get some education. Then he can come back to the farm.'

'Well, there's something in what you say . . .' the old man said.

'And who knows, maybe Tommy will turn out to have more brains than us, and he'll be . . . well, I don't know. A rich man, maybe. If we give him an education.'

The old man nodded, and his wife, seeing that she had persuaded him, said nothing more about it, but crooned, 'Pretty, pretty, pretty,' to the little ginger cat that purred on her lap.

Now, when the old couple's neighbours heard about this, they all had a good laugh, and the news went round the village in no time at all. The way the old couple treated the kitten they'd taken in had been causing comment for some time. 'A good many children don't get treated so well,' people would say; and, 'They talk to it as if it was going to answer back.'

'But,' said others, 'it's really no laughing matter. Somebody should stop them before they make fools of themselves.'

After all, a lot of people make pets of dogs and cats and talk to them, and about them, as if they were people. But when they start planning to have them educated, it's time something was done.

The first neighbour brave enough to go up to the farm about the matter didn't do well. As soon as she started trying to explain that the little cat was only a cat, and couldn't be educated, the old woman got very hoity-toity. 'I'll thank you to mind your own affairs and leave us to mind ours,' she said. 'If we choose to educate our child, what's that to you, if you please?'

Others who tried to make the old couple see sense did no better. The old couple said to each other, 'They're jealous, that's what they are. Jealous that our little Tommy's going to have a proper education, and their children aren't.'

And very soon after that, the old man said to his wife, 'Wrap Tommy up well, and let's go and see the Vicar.'

2

A Kitten's Education

The old woman ran for her shawl and bonnet, and she put Tommy into a soft cloth bag with a drawstring neck, so she could carry him without his jumping from her arms and running away. Their neighbours watched them go, and tut-tutted, and wondered what would come of it. Nothing good, they said, nothing good.

The old couple, carrying the struggling little cat, walked all the way to the next village, and to the little house beside the church where the Vicar lived.

Tommy mewed and wailed all the way: he didn't like being carried and he didn't like being taken from home. 'Oh, don't you want to leave us, Tommy?' said the old woman. 'We'll miss you too, but never mind, there'll be holidays, and it's for the best. Now shush, shush, don't cry.'

They were shown in by the Vicar's housekeeper, and they sat on the Vicar's hard chairs, feeling shy, with the old woman holding the wriggling, miauling cat on her lap.

The Vicar, when he came into the room, was a tall and rather plump man, who looked nice enough. 'How can I help you?' he asked, sounding very bored.

The old man put out his hand to stroke the cat's head and said, 'Please, Master, we'd like you to educate our son.'

'Your son?' said the Vicar, looking round for a boy.

'Yes, little Tommy here,' said the old man, while his wife looked shyly at the floor. 'If you would be so good, sir.'

The Vicar realised that they meant the cat, and he felt like laughing, but then he thought it would be a better joke if he took things on a bit further. So he kept his face serious and asked, 'What do you want me to teach him?'

'Well ... you know about that, sir; I don't. Reading and writing, and everything that's educational, sir.'

'This son?' asked the Vicar, just to make sure, and pointed at the cat on the old woman's lap.

'Yes, sir; our only son,' said the old man. 'So we want to do everything we can for him. We'll pay, of course.'

Now, if the old man hadn't said that, the Vicar would have laughed at them, and turned them out of his house. But when he heard mention of payment, he changed his mind. 'It would be very expensive,' he said. 'You'd have to pay for his bed and board here, and for all his books and paper and ink; and for his clothes.'

'We'll manage, sir.'

'For three years,' said the Vicar.

'Three years!' exclaimed the old woman, who had not thought she would be parted from her little Thomas for so long.

'That is the usual period of schooling,' said the Vicar, and then thought of a way of making sure he was never found out. 'Those three years will be devoted to study,' he said. 'He will live here with me all the time: no holidays, no visits. I have found that holidays and visits only distract the scholars from their lessons and make them homesick. They do much better without them.'

'Three years, and not to see him in all that time!' said the old woman.

'It is best,' said the Vicar.

'And you know best, sir, I'm sure,' said the old man. 'We don't like it, but if you say that's how it must be, then that's how it must be.'

The Vicar got up from his seat, took the cat from the old woman, and began to stroke its head. 'I know just how to look after him, so you mustn't worry. Leave him here with me now, and I'll begin his education immediately.'

'But what about payment?' asked the old man.

'Oh, I'll call on you for that,' said the Vicar. 'It's better that I should call on you to collect it than that you should come here. If Tommy were to see you, he might be upset.'

The old couple stood up. They knew they were doing the right thing for Tommy, but they were still unhappy. The old man took his wife's hand. 'But how much will it be, sir?' he asked. 'I want to know so I can have the money ready for you.'

'Let me see,' said the Vicar, and made calculations in his mind. 'Three hundred pounds a year.'

'Three hundred pounds a year!' cried the old woman, and gripped her husband's hand in both of hers. 'In money?' It was a great amount of money for them to find every year for three years.

'That is rather cheap, in fact,' said the Vicar sternly. 'You would pay far more to anyone but me – but I'm a fool to myself, and always ready to help people if I can. I'm just made that way. So all I ask you to pay me is three hundred pounds a year, and if you don't always have the money, I'm sure we could come to some arrangement. You can pay me in eggs or butter or whatever you have.'

'Oh thank you, thank you!' the old couple said. 'That's very, very kind of you.'

'Now go quickly!' said the Vicar. 'No kisses and goodbyes, please! It will only upset Tommy, and you don't want to do that, do you?' And he hustled the old couple out of his house as quickly as he could.

They walked all the way home in tears. The old woman cried openly, but the old man tried to hide his grief for a long time, before finding the effort too much, and letting the tears run. They walked with their arms around each other, and they said, again and again, 'But it's for the best. He'll thank us when he's older, and doing well. What's three years, after all? It'll soon pass, and then he'll be home again.'

People passing them on the road stared, and some asked what was the matter.

'We've left our son to be educated and we won't see him for three years,' said the old man.

'Oh never mind, cheer up!' said the passers-by. 'Three years will fly past.' And some, who knew the old couple, would start to laugh once they'd passed them, and to say to their friends: 'That's the mad old pair who think their kitten is their son! There's no telling them it's only a cat – and, well, if it makes them happy, what harm is there in it?'

Once they reached home, the old couple had to begin making plans. 'However will we raise all that money every year?' asked the old woman.

'We'll just have to, that's all,' said the old man. 'I'll have to work harder.'

'But you can't grow any more to a field than the field will give,' said the old woman. '*I'll* have to work harder: I'll have to make more butter and cheese and sell it. We'll have to eat less, old man, so there's more to sell.'

'Oh well, we've had our life,' said the old man. 'It's Tommy's life that matters now. Eating a bit less won't hurt us – I'm getting fat!'

But how was the Vicar getting on with the education of Tommy? How do you teach a kitten its alphabet or its multiplication tables? Will it put up its paw politely to answer questions? Will it secretly eat mice in class?

Tommy's education was very short. As soon as the old couple were out of sight, the Vicar wrang Tommy's neck and killed him, without even taking him from the drawstring bag; and then he threw the kitten's body into an old, dry well at the bottom of the Vicarage garden. And he laughed to himself about the stupid old pair who thought that a cat was their son, and that a cat could be educated. Such fools, he thought, deserved to be cheated.

But he went to the farm to collect the money for

educating Tommy, four times a year for three years. Every time he went there, the old couple received him with thanks, because they were so grateful to him, and they gave him the best of everything they had to eat and drink. He always told them that their Tommy was doing wonderfully well at his books, and was amused by how pleased and proud they were to hear this news. What idiots they are, he thought. He noticed, as time went on, how much thinner the old people became, and how worn their clothes; and he noticed that the farm-house became shabby and ill-repaired, while more and more of the farm-land about it was ploughed and worked and well-cared for. But the Vicar had never worked hard for his living, and didn't know or care how hard the old couple were working, and for what long hours; he didn't care how far they were travelling to markets, or how little they were eating while they saved every penny to pay him. If they'd a brain in their heads, he thought, they would never have fallen for his trick; but since they hadn't a brain between them, why should he worry about them? God helps those who help themselves.

What did the Vicar do with the money that the old couple paid him? Well, some he spent on expensive wine and food, and books; but some he spent on presents for more powerful churchmen than himself. That made them notice him, and he won promotion, and, at the end of the three years, he moved away from the little village to a large town, where he was rather more important than before.

But he went back to the farm to see the old couple. 'I want to go on educating your son,' he said. 'He is brilliant! The best pupil I ever had. Let me teach him for three more years, and then he can go to University and might do anything! He might enter the church and become a bishop – or he might be a lawyer – or a doctor. You won't say no, will you?'

The old couple blushed and beamed with pride. They had never dared to hope that their Tommy might be so clever. A bishop! A doctor! 'We can't say no, can we, mother?' said the old man. 'If our Tommy's doing that well, let him go on, I say!'

'But couldn't he come home for a holiday, sir?' the old woman asked.

'Oh yes, let him come home and see us for a while,' agreed her husband.

'That would be a great mistake,' said the priest. 'Tommy misses you and speaks of you often, but you'd see what would happen if he came home – you'd spoil him so much that he wouldn't want to go back to his studies, and would never do the great things he might do.'

'That's true, old woman,' said the old man. 'You know we would spoil him; we'd ruin him.'

'But I only want Tommy to be happy,' said the

old woman. 'If he doesn't want to study any more, let him come home. I don't care if he's not a lawyer, if he doesn't want to be.'

'Oh, that's true too,' said the old man. 'I never wanted him to be anything but a farmer like me. If he wants to be a lawyer, or something like that, well enough, but if he's not happy, sir, if he wants to come home – then let him come, that's what I say.'

'No, no,' said the Vicar. 'He is quite happy at the moment; he is used to his life. But let him stop for a holiday now, and he will change his mind; I've seen it happen to students again and again. Think of his future! After spending so much money on his education, surely you want him to do as well as he can?'

'Oh yes. Yes, we want him to have all the things we never had,' said the old couple, though they didn't even know what those things were. The Vicar soon persuaded them that the best thing for Tommy was to let him study for another three years without a holiday.

'Of course, now that I'm living in the town, it will cost me more to keep Tommy,' said the Vicar, 'and the books he will need will be more expensive. I hate to ask you for more money – you know me, I'm so soft-hearted – I wish I could teach Tommy for nothing, he's such a bright little chap – but you know how it is. Money doesn't grow on trees. I shall need five hundred pounds a year now.'

'Five hundred pounds! We can't pay it!' the old woman whispered, but her husband said, 'We'll pay the money, don't you worry, sir. We know you wouldn't ask for it if you didn't have to. Just you look after our Tommy and keep him at his books.'

'Oh, I will,' said the Vicar, and went away.

'How shall we ever find five hundred pounds a year?' the old woman asked.

'We didn't think we could find three hundred,' said the old man, 'but we did. We'll manage. Perhaps he'll take more of it in eggs and bacon and such.'

Four times every year for the next three years, the Vicar sent a messenger to the old people to collect the money they owed him. Every time the messenger arrived the old couple were thinner, and more exhausted than before. Their whole life was work and worry; up before dawn, and never stopping while there was light. The old woman did washing for her neighbours, and stitched clothing, besides all her other work, just to earn a few shillings; the old man delivered messages and parcels and ploughed other people's fields besides his own. They ate only the poorest food and little of that, putting away every penny they could earn to pay Tommy's school fees.

Their neighbours, seeing what was happening, felt sorry for them, and often tried to help. They felt guilty for not stopping the Vicar from taking the old people's money – but what could they do? The old couple wouldn't hear a word said against the Vicar, and were never happier than when talking about how well their Tommy was doing. 'It's awful,' said the neighbours to each other, 'but if we could make them believe that they're being swindled, they'd be even more unhappy than they were before.'

'We can only hope it'll turn out for the best,' someone else would say.

'Yes; but how can it? No education goes on forever. What happens when it's time for Tommy to come home?'

The old couple went on working towards the time when Tommy's lessons would all be learned. 'Only three more years, and then we shall see him,' they said to each other, and worked, and looked forward to the time when they could say, 'Only two more years.' And then they worked until they could say, 'Only one more year.'

At the end of that last year the Vicar himself came to see them. The old couple had been watching for him and, when they saw him coming, they hurried out to meet him, as fast as their old legs would carry them. But the Vicar seemed to be alone. Where was Tommy? Perhaps he had strayed away from the Vicar's side to play in the fields and woods.

'Where is our Tommy, Vicar?' the old woman panted out, as soon as they were near enough.

'Isn't he here, with you?' the Vicar asked, surprised – or pretending to be.

'No,' said the old man. 'When we saw you, we thought you were bringing him home at last.'

'I'm afraid not,' said the Vicar. 'I have some sad news for you. Tommy didn't come down to breakfast yesterday, and when I went to his room to fetch him, he wasn't there. He had run away. Of course, I thought he would come here; but if he hasn't . . .'

'Oh, where can he be?' cried the old woman. 'Oh, my little Tommy, what's happened to him?'

'I imagine,' said the Vicar, 'that he has run away to sea. He has been talking about the sea and ships a good deal just lately. He didn't want to enter the church, or become a lawyer or a doctor.'

'Oh no, oh no,' cried the old woman, and sat down on the ground in the lane. 'All these years

I've worked and worked, thinking I'd see him again at the end of it – but now he'll be drowned! The ship'll sink and he'll be drowned and I'll never see him again!'

'He might not, he might not,' said the old man, bending over her. 'Look on the bright side, Mother. He might come back to us, yet. He just wants a bit of adventure, and then he'll come home and settle down.'

'With an arm or a leg missing!' the old woman wailed.

And so the Vicar left them, because he didn't think he could keep himself from laughing for much longer. The old couple went sadly home, and hardly knew how to live for their disappointment. They stopped the work they'd been doing, except for feeding and milking their animals, for what was the point of working now there was no Tommy to work for?

Their neighbours were sad for them, and said among themselves, 'You see, no good could come of it; no good at all.' But they had never been able to persuade the old people that their kitten was not a child; and it had seemed cruel to even try. It would be even crueller, now, they thought; and so they told the old couple how sorry they were that Tommy had been so thoughtless as to run away, and said that they hoped he would soon return home safe.

3

The Vicar's Little Joke

While the old couple were so sad, the Vicar was doing very well in the town, with the help of the money the old people had paid him; so well that, within three more years he was promoted again and had to leave for London. But before he left, he decided to play one last joke on the old couple.

He made up an advertisement, and paid for it to be placed in a newspaper. When it was printed, he bought a copy of the newspaper and took it with him to the farm. The old couple greeted him sadly, but they were still grateful to him, and did their best to be hospitable.

'Look at this,' he said, and showed them the advertisement he had made up, and then, because they could not read well, he read it aloud to them.

'It says,' said he, '*Master Thomas Katt, Merchant, having left the shores of Russia and put in at the port of London, is residing at The Miching Mouse Inn and is available to all those wishing to buy the Wares of Muscovy.* Now that,' said the Vicar, 'can only be your Thomas. He ran away to sea, but the education I gave him was so good that he has risen to be a merchant-captain already. You should go and see him.'

'Yes!' cried the old couple, and reached for each other's hands. 'Yes, we must, we shall! Thank you, sir, thank you for coming out of your way to tell us – you are so good to us!'

The Vicar left for London by coach, and, all the way there, he laughed at the thought of the old couple making the long, hard journey, without any of his comforts, and then finding, at the end of it, that there was no Miching Mouse Inn, and no Mr. Thomas Katt, Merchant. Fools to the end, he thought. Serves them right.

The old couple asked a neighbour to look after their farm while they travelled to London. He tried to persuade them not to go, but they wouldn't listen to him. What little money they had, the old woman sewed into the seams and hems of their clothes, until they were so heavy they could hardly move. Then they begged a ride on a cart and they travelled, slowly, with much bumping and bruising of their old bones, to London.

When the cart entered London, it carried them through more streets, and past more houses than they had ever seen. There was so much noise in the streets that they couldn't hear each other when they spoke: it was all from people shouting, and from iron horse-shoes and iron wheel-rims on stones. The cart stopped, and they climbed down, to be pushed and shoved from every side. There was nowhere they could stand and be safe from the crowd. They huddled close together for a long time, holding hands, and not knowing which way to go, before the old woman found the courage to put out her hand and catch the arm of a girl who was hurrying by with a basket of vegetables.

'Begging your pardon, miss – can you tell us the way to the Miching Mouse Inn?'

'The Miching Mouse? Oh yes! You go ...' But then the girl looked at the shy old couple, and knew that they could never remember all the turnings and landmarks she would have to tell them. 'I'm going past there myself,' she said, though she wasn't. 'I'll take you to it.'

'Oh, thank you, thank you!' said the old couple, and gratefully went with the girl, through a bewilderment of streets and passages. It was so dangerous to cross the roads, where the carts and carriages never ceased to pass, that it took all their concentration, and they could remember nothing of the way they had come. But the girl brought them, after a long and frightening walk, to a street of fine buildings, and to the door of an inn with white stone steps, and white pillars at the door. Over the door swung a painted sign, showing a crouching mouse with a piece of cheese. 'Here's the Miching Mouse,' said the girl. 'Hope you find your son.' For the old couple had gasped out the reason for their visit as they had hurried along behind her.

'And thank you, my dear,' they said, shaking

her hand. The girl smiled and ran away, in a hurry to make up the time she had lost in guiding them.

The old couple were left looking at the beautiful steps and door of the inn. They had not realised before how grubby and shabby were their clothes and shoes, but now they were timid about climbing those steps and leaving dusty footmarks on them. Such a grand place, and such grand people must be inside – they certainly would not want a grubby old pair like them to join them.

'Our Tommy must have done well for himself to be staying here,' whispered the old woman to the old man.

'Perhaps he won't want us to come showing him up,' said the old man. 'He'll be ashamed of us. Maybe we'd better go home, and wait for him to come to us.'

'What? Go home when we've come this far? And I'll tell you something, old man, if Tommy's ashamed of us after all we've done for him, I'm ashamed of Tommy! If he doesn't want to see us when we've come all this way, then I never want to see him again!'

And the old woman marched up the steps of the inn and through its open door; and the old man had to run after her.

But once inside the inn all the old woman's courage went away, it was such a fine place: polished floors, and polished wooden panelling;

paintings and shining candlesticks. There was a bar, all hung with shining pewter cups and glasses. The old couple stood just inside the door, wondering if they ought to scuttle out again, before someone came and threw them out.

'We could stand here 'til the cows come home,' the old man whispered. 'We must ask!'

'Then you ask,' said the old woman, giving him a push. 'I asked the way.'

The old man took his wife's hand and went bravely up to the bar. When the man behind it looked at him, the old man coughed and said loudly, 'I'm looking for Mr. Thomas Katt, Merchant.'

'Just put in from the shores of Russia,' added the old woman.

The barman looked at them hard. 'What would *you* want with him?'

'We're his parents!' said the old man. 'Come up from the country to see him.'

The barman's face changed to smiles. 'His parents. Ah, well – you'll find Mr. Katt in the dining room, over there, sir. Just go straight in, please.'

The old couple hurried, hand in hand to the door of the dining room, and stopped. 'Oh, just think!' cried the old woman, squeezing her husband's hand. 'In a minute we shall see our Tommy!'

4

The Merchant

From the dining room they could hear the clink of cutlery on plates, and the ring of glasses; the soft sound of many voices talking quietly. They peeped through the open door and saw a long table spread with a beautiful cloth, and surrounded by many people dressed in much better clothes than the ones the old couple were wearing. 'Can you see Tommy?' the old man asked.

'No – oh yes! There he is, look, there he is!' The old woman pointed and there indeed, at the table, quite near them, sat their Tommy. The old woman had recognised him at once, and, when he was pointed out, so did the old man. Their little kitten had grown into a stocky, handsome little man, with the same red hair that he had always had, and a broad-cheeked, narrow-chinned face. His eyes were green and slanting, and would give away to anyone the fact that he had once been a cat. And over the back of his chair hung a cloak with a lining of orange-yellow, tabby-patterned silk.

Now they could see their Tommy, the old couple had more courage, and they went to his side.

'Tommy!' said the old woman. 'Oh, my lovely little kittie!' And she bent down and kissed the red-haired man, who was startled.

The old man thumped the red-head on the shoulders and said, 'Tommy you bad lad, why did you run away and worry your mother like that? If you wanted to go to sea, why didn't you come home and see us first?'

'Oh, don't shout at him, old man, not now we've found him,' said the old woman. 'Oh Tommy, you have grown; you look hardly anything like a cat anymore!'

Now, the red-headed man was, in fact, named Mr. Thomas Katt, but he had never seen the two old people before in his life, and he couldn't understand why they should be making such a fuss of him, and causing everyone else in the dining room to stare. He tried to tell the old couple that they had mistaken him for someone else, but he couldn't make them listen; and soon he was more interested in listening to them. They knew his name; they knew that he had just put into port from Russia, and they called him their son. They must be mad, he thought, but all the same, he was curious about them. He gave his seat at the table to the old woman, fetched other chairs for himself and the old man, and called to the inn servant to bring plates and food for his mother and father.

'Oh, I don't know that we can afford to eat here – can we old woman?' said the old man.

'But I shall be paying,' said Mr. Thomas Katt.

'Did you have a good journey here?'

And so he heard all about their journey, and the
girl who had directed them, and the money they
had sewn into their clothes. 'It's all for you,
Tommy; you know what to do with money better
than we do,' said the old woman.

Mr. Thomas Katt was interested at the
mention of money; all merchants can find a use for
ready cash at any time. But he said, 'How did you
know where to find me?'

And then he heard about the Vicar, and the advertisement in the newspaper. 'Ah,' said Mr. Katt,
but he knew there was some trick because, at the
time the Vicar had shown the old couple the advertisement, he had still been on the sea, and had not
placed an advertisement in any newspaper.

So Mr. Thomas Katt ordered more wine, and
filled the glasses of his guests, while drinking very
little himself; and he listened as the old couple

became talkative and sentimental, and remembered the old days, when he had been just a kitten. The old woman wept a little as she remembered how they had taken him to be educated by the Vicar; and then smiled again as she and the old man laughingly told of how hard they had worked to pay the schooling fees.

Mr. Thomas Katt was a clever man: he said little, but listened hard, and he soon pieced together most of the story. 'The old people are a little mad,' he thought, 'but they are good people all the same, and they have been cheated. And if they think I'm their kitten grown into a man, so, by Heaven, I shall be.'

Mr. Thomas Katt ordered a room at the Miching Mouse Inn for his new parents. It made them shy when they saw it; for this single room held more fine furniture and materials than the whole of their old farm house.

'Oh, Tommy, I shall never dare to sit on them chairs in my old clothes, for fear I should dirty 'em,' said the old woman.

'We can't have that,' said Thomas Katt, and he sent out for a dressmaker and a tailor, and ordered new clothes for the old couple. 'I shall pay,' he said when he saw they were afraid of the cost. 'But until the clothes come, Mother, you mustn't be afraid of sitting down; this is your room, your chairs, your bed. Believe me, the parents of Thomas Katt can do no wrong at the Miching Mouse.'

'Ooh, are you so important then, Tommy?' the old woman asked.

'Important? No,' said Thomas Katt. 'But I pay my bills like an honest man, and I keep my word – and here, Mother, have this from me, to make up for all the years I've been away.' And he took, from his hat, a large brooch, made of enamelled gold with hanging pearls. The old woman's eyes and mouth opened wide. 'That was given me,' said Thomas Katt, 'by the Czar of Russia, for bringing him letters from our Queen. And here, Father.' From his thumb, Thomas Katt took a large gold ring set with rubies and gave it to the old man. 'That was a present from our Queen, for taking her letters to the Czar.'

'The Queen gave you a present?' said the old woman in a whisper, while the old man stared at the ring.

'That's not the only present she's given me . . . You see, Mother, your years of hard work and saving weren't wasted. I'm a rich man now, and I shall pay you back for everything.' And he sat with them, and told them stories of Russia, and Spain, of Italy, France, Denmark and the New Americas until they were dazed with astonishment and couldn't be surprised any more. Then he left them to go to bed, and went to his own room.

The old couple were tired out and, despite the big, soft, comfortable bed they climbed into, unlike any bed they had ever known before, they were soon fast and happily asleep. But Thomas Katt lay awake a long time, missing the sea, and thinking over all that had happened to him that day. For this Mr. Thomas Katt was an orphan. His parents had died when he had been so young that he could remember nothing about them; and he had been brought up in a home for poor boys. There he had been taught to read, write and reckon, and at the age of ten, he had been sent to earn his living on board ship. He had grown up to be a sailor, and had helped to capture Spanish ships for the Queen. With his share of the prize-money, he had become a merchant, and had made himself rich. But all his life he had wondered who his parents had been, and had wished that he had a family; and now, by this strange chance, he had a mother and a father.

And the old couple had a loving son, for

Thomas did all he could to please them. He took them to the theatre, and bought them pig's feet and marzipan to eat while they watched the murders and ghosts on the stage. He took them to the warehouse, where the goods he had brought from Muscovy were stored, and showed them furs, and amber, and made them a present of a jar of caviar. He took them on board his ship, which thrilled them, for they had never seen a ship before, or the sea, and at the end of the day they felt quite weak and giddy with excitement. He took them to the cathedral of St. Paul's, and to the bookshops outside it, and showed them how well he could read. He bought them new clothes, and expensive treats such as sugar and tea, and strange orange fruits they had never seen before. And he bought a small, pretty house for them to live in.

'I always meant to buy a house one day,' he said. 'Now I have bought it, and you shall keep it for me while I'm at sea.'

The old couple were so pleased with the house that they were forever walking about it, and rattling up and down the stairs, to view all the rooms again; and when they were exhausted, they would sit, each in their own armchair, looking at each other and unable to stop smiling at how well things had turned out, despite their disappointment when Tommy had run away to sea. The house was perfect, for Thomas had been careful to ensure that it had a garden where vegetables could be grown, a sty where a pig could be kept, and a yard for chickens, so that the old people wouldn't miss their country life.

But they were worried about their farm. 'I am a merchant by trade, and a sailor at heart,' said Thomas. 'I could never be a farmer; but, if you agree, Mother, Father, I'll ride down there, and rent out the farm, so the land doesn't go to waste.'

At first the old couple were doubtful, but then they decided that they would like to try town life for a while. Indeed, living with Thomas, they were already growing fatter and more inclined to sit with their feet up than to plough or scrub. So they agreed, and Mr. Thomas Katt left them in town, and rode to their village.

The villagers were much astonished by the arrival of this fine, red-haired gentleman, who wore a long, dangling pearl in his ear and a silk-lined cloak on his back, and who introduced himself as the son of the old couple who had left their farm and gone up to London. The villagers knew very well that the old couple hadn't a son, but only a kitten; and yet this Mr. Thomas Katt had papers, official looking papers, signed and sealed, saying that he was the old couple's son, and had every right to rent out their farm. People stared at Thomas Katt whenever they saw him, and followed him about, to get a better look at him. No one had the nerve to ask him what it had been like to be a cat, though everyone wondered.

When Mr. Thomas Katt had settled the arrangements about the renting of his parent's land, he went along to the next village, to visit the Vicar there.

'I want to ask you about the Vicar who was here before you,' said Mr. Katt. 'What was his name, and where has he gone? I need to find him.'

'Oh, I don't know much about him,' said the new Vicar. 'He wasn't much liked by all accounts – but my housekeeper used to keep house for him too. Why don't you ask her about him?'

The housekeeper remembered the old Vicar well. She remembered letting in the old couple with the kitten, and she remembered seeing the Vicar throw something down the well later that same day. And so Mr. Thomas Katt climbed down into the old dry well at the bottom of the Vicarage garden, while the housekeeper and the new Vicar watched him from above.

The well was filled with rubbish, and dead leaves, but Mr. Katt dug determinedly into it, never minding how he dirtied his good clothes; and then the two watching saw that he had found something he wanted. He stood still at the bottom of the well, examining whatever it was.

'What's that you've found there?' the new Vicar called.

Mr. Thomas Katt looked up and smiled. 'Help me out, and I'll show you!'

So the Vicar and the housekeeper helped him to climb out of the well, and when he was safely on level ground again, he put what he had found on the wall of the well. It was a filthy old bag, a little rotted; its neck drawn tightly closed with strings.

Mr. Thomas Katt opened the bag carefully and showed them what was inside.

'Bones,' said the housekeeper. 'What is it?'

'My little brother,' said Thomas Katt, and they wondered if he was right in the head. 'Tell me,' said Thomas Katt, looking up at them, 'would you like to come up to London and see the Queen, you, Madam, and you, Vicar?'

The two looked at each other in amazement.

'I shall pay all expenses, of course,' said Master Thomas Katt.

5

The Queen's Chaplain

So when Thomas Katt returned to town, he took with him, in a box, the drawstring bag, and the bones inside it; and, in a coach, the Vicar and his housekeeper.

In London, he found rooms for his guests at an inn, for he did not want to take them home, where they might meet his parents and give things away. After seeing his guests housed, he went away and made more enquiries. He found that the Vicar who had made the old couple pay for the education of their kitten was now the Chaplain of the Queen's own chapel! And people said what a good man he was, and how hard he worked for the poor. But Thomas Katt asked more questions, and more, and he found that the Queen's Chaplain was not as good as he seemed. The money he collected for the poor was not spent on the poor at all, but paid for the Chaplain's musicians and books and wine. And what was more, the Chaplain hardly ever paid what he owed to his tailors and his jewellers.

'Well, sir,' thought Thomas to himself, 'I am a merchant, and I like to see bills paid – and I think I owe you something for my education.'

Now Mr. Thomas Katt dressed in his best and

went to the Court, where he asked permission to speak to the Queen privately; and he was such a favourite with her, that she only made him wait two days. And when he got to see her at last, he invited her to a grand dinner he was to give: 'For I want to make Your Majesty some return for the favour you did me in choosing me to carry your letters to the Czar,' he said.

The Queen asked who else was to be at the dinner.

'Oh, your Chaplain,' said Thomas. 'I hear everywhere what a good man he is; and your secretary, Madam, that good old man, has said he will come – and my good friends, the captains of *The Pelican* and *The Good Fortune*.'

'Fine company,' said the Queen. 'My Chaplain is a most charming, amusing man. Make the meal as good, Thomas, and I shall certainly be there.'

So Thomas took the best room at the Miching Mouse Inn, and ordered the finest meal ever cooked in the kitchens there. He wanted the dinner to be a success, because he had a plan. When his guests were at ease, and talking freely, he meant to lead the Chaplain into confessing the trick he had played on the old couple. The captains arrived first, dressed in their best. Then came the Royal party: the Chaplain, smiling and full of soft, polite words to thank Thomas Katt for inviting him; the Secretary, tall and quiet, and the Queen, a long dark cloak covering her splendid dress, so she should not be noticed.

The dinner was excellent, and the talk was as good, for Thomas told of his adventures in Russia, and how he had hunted wolves with the Czar and been lost in the snow; while the captain of *The Pelican* told how he had been shipwrecked; and the captain of *The Good Fortune* told of a land he had visited where the people had no heads, but kept their eyes and mouths in their chests. And then the Queen proposed a toast to the success of trade, which they all gladly drank, but which reminded Thomas of how he had once been cheated and made a fine fool. So he told that story.

'It cost me a lot of money,' he said, 'to learn that not all men can be trusted, however respectable their dress and however kindly their words.'

The other captains laughed at him and at his story, but were quick to tell stories of how they had been cheated too; and even the Queen's Secretary could tell a story of how, when he had been a little boy, he had been persuaded to swap his shoes for a penknife which, when he tried to use it, proved to be broken.

'But I've done some cheating too, in my time,' said the captain of *The Good Fortune*, and told how he had got the better of a French merchant. Thomas Katt and the captain of *The Pelican* matched him with tales of how successful they had been, too, on many occasions, in cheating those who were trying to cheat them. The Queen pronounced herself finely entertained, and drank a toast to all her merchants and all her captains, but especially those present.

'What, no toast for your Churchmen?' asked Thomas, smiling at the Royal Chaplain. 'Tell us of your doings, Master Cleric, and earn yourself a toast!'

'Oh,' said the Queen's Chaplain, 'I have not spent my life in travelling and trading, but in quiet study ... and yet, I remember, when I was just a poor, country parson ...' And, to show that he could entertain the Queen as well as any merchant-captain, and to boast of how clever and cunning he was, the Chaplain began to tell of how an old farmer and his wife had come to him one day, and had asked him to educate their kitten! 'How could I make them unhappy by telling them that their darling was a cat and not a child?' he said. 'I took the kitten, and their money, and when they were gone from my door, I wrung the kitten's neck and threw its carcass down my old well – so I never spent even a penny on its keep!'

The Chaplain went on with his tale, laughing himself at how the old people worked themselves to shadows, and how they listened with all their ears to the stories he made up about their kitten: and most of all he laughed at how he had invented the advertisement, and sent the old fools running off to London to search for an inn and a merchant that didn't exist. 'Heaven knows what became of them!' said the Chaplain, tears of laughter running from his eyes. 'They came looking for Mr. Thomas Katt at the Miching Mouse Inn – whoever heard of such names? Who but fools would believe in them?'

'But Chaplain,' said Thomas, 'we are sitting in the Miching Mouse Inn; and my name is Thomas Katt.'

Then the Chaplain realised that no one was laughing with him, but all were looking at him with distaste; and he blushed and felt uncomfortable.

'Well, what a coincidence, eh?' he said, and laughed again. But still no one else laughed, and so he soon stopped. He felt that he had been made to look a fool before the Queen, and he blamed Thomas Katt for that. He looked across the table at Master Katt, with his showy clothes and pearl earring, and he began to hate him. He was quiet for the rest of the evening, the better to watch Thomas Katt, and hate him, and think of some way of being revenged on him.

The next day, Thomas Katt went to see the Queen again, taking with him a box. 'Did Your Majesty enjoy my dinner party?' he asked.

'Very much, Thomas; you must ask me to another.'

'And was Your Majesty entertained by the stories told?'

The Queen frowned. 'All but that told by my Chaplain. A cruel and unpleasant tale I thought that.'

'It was no tale,' said Thomas, 'but the truth,' and he opened the box and showed the bones and skull of the little kitten, and the draw-string bag that had been its shroud. And Thomas told how the old couple, when they had come to the city on their fool's errand, had found their way to him, and how he had felt sorry for them, and had let them think that they were indeed his parents. 'But it angers me, Your Majesty, that the man who cheated the old couple should go unpunished.'

'But Thomas, how can I believe this?' asked the Queen. 'It's a joke, surely?'

'No joke, Your Majesty,' said Thomas, and he called forward the Vicar from the country, and his housekeeper, and they told the Queen how her Chaplain had once been the Vicar in their village, and how he had been brought a kitten one day, and had strangled it and thrown it into the well. 'And I saw Master Katt climb down that well and bring up those bones,' said the housekeeper, pointing to the kitten's skeleton.

'Send for my Chaplain,' said the Queen.

The Chaplain was surprised and anxious when he was told that the Queen wished to see him. He could think of no reason why she should, and it worried him. He went to his mirror, and made sure that he looked his best, and then he picked up his prayer-book and hurried through the palace corridors.

When he arrived at the audience room, he found the Queen in a bad temper. The toe of her embroidered shoe tapped on the floor, and her ringed fingers rapped on the arms of her chair. Her face was scowling. Something, thought the Chaplain, has gone very badly wrong; something has annoyed Her Majesty. He did hope it wasn't him.

But then he saw that Master Thomas Katt was in the room, dressed, as usual, in showy silks and velvets. Perhaps it was Master Katt who had angered the Queen?

'Chaplain,' said the Queen. 'I want your

advice. I am so angry, I cannot trust my own judgement. Suppose you had gone to a man of good reputation, a man said to be honest and trustworthy . . .' As she said this, the Queen looked at Thomas Katt, and scowled.

The Chaplain almost smiled. She is speaking of our fine Master Katt, he thought to himself. It *is* he who has annoyed her!

'Suppose,' said the Queen, 'you had entrusted to this man the thing you valued most in the world. Suppose you begged him to take good care of it. And suppose this man, whom you trusted, destroyed your treasure, and stole from you besides, all the time pretending to be your friend, and laughing at you because you were foolish enough to trust him.' And again the Queen glowered at Thomas Katt.

Oh, thought the Chaplain gleefully, Her Majesty has trusted Master Katt to fetch some gift from abroad, and he has cheated her of it. Good, good! The Chaplain was pleased that he was going to see Thomas Katt punished. That will teach him to try and make me look foolish, he thought.

'What would you do with such a man, Chaplain?' the Queen asked. Now the Chaplain was more delighted than ever! Not only was he going to see this man, whom he hated, punished, but he was going to have the pleasure of choosing the punishment. But he pulled his mouth straight from the smile it was curving into, and looked at the cover of his prayer book. He made his face sad and gentle. 'Such a betrayal of trust is a wicked, wicked thing,' he said sadly. 'It deserves the very harshest of punishments.'

'I agree,' said the Queen, 'but what punishment?'

The Chaplain looked sideways at Thomas Katt. 'I think he should be stripped of all the fine clothes he wears to please people's eyes. Then I think he should be whipped through the streets with a crier to tell people what he has done. Then I think he should be hanged. And serve him right!'

'Excellent, Chaplain,' said the Queen. 'That is what shall be done with you.'

The Chaplain jumped. He looked up and saw that the Queen was no longer scowling at Thomas Katt, but at him. 'What?'

'You have named your own punishment,' said the Queen. 'You it was who took from the old couple their greatest treasure, their little kitten; you it was who killed the kitten, and robbed them of their living, year by year. And it is you who shall be stripped of your church robes, whipped through the streets and hung.'

The Chaplain knelt, not in prayer, but because his legs were weak. He thought of what the crowds in the street would say when they learned what he had done; how they would shout and spit and strike at him. He shuddered with fear, but could not find his voice to ask forgiveness. And then, he thought, I shall be hung! He put his hands over his face.

'Have you nothing to say for yourself?' the Queen asked.

The Chaplain took his hands from his face. He knew that if he was to save his life, he must make an effort now. 'Please, Your Majesty, please, please, don't do this to me!'

'You had no such pity on the old couple you tormented and robbed,' said the Queen. 'Why should pity be shown to you?'

'But, Your Majesty – I didn't do them any harm! I made them happy! They wished to spend their money on educating their kitten – I helped them!'

'You made them happy, sir, you helped them! Do you suppose I might believe that? Do you dare to think me a fool? Because of you they went hungry and ragged, because of you they had sleepless nights of worry – do you tell me that is what made them happy? Do you dare to tell me that, sir?'

'No, no,' said the priest miserably. 'But – I'm not entirely to blame! They shouldn't have fallen for my trick! I could not have caught you out, Your Majesty, or the good Master Katt; you are both too clever; and so . . .'

The Queen rose from her chair, her fists clenched and her face flushing with rage. 'You make me angry!' she shouted and, bending down, she pulled off her shoe and threw it at the Chaplain. It hit him on the head and made a sore place. 'Do you expect me, then, to find the innocent guilty of innocence, and the trusting guilty of trust?' the Queen yelled. 'The law says, *Thou shalt not steal*; it does not say *Thou shalt not be a fool*. And my laws shall ever protect the foolish and the trusting from the liars and the cheats. No, do not speak to me again, sir! You shall hang, sir, you shall hang!'

The Chaplain began to shake all over with fear and he covered his face again; so he didn't see Thomas Katt go down on one knee. 'Madam,' said Thomas Katt, 'may I ask for mercy on your Chaplain's behalf?'

'There shall be no mercy for him!' said the Queen.

'But I know a more severe punishment, Madam.'

'More severe than hanging?'

The Chaplain began to listen.

Mr. Thomas Katt said, 'Your Highness; to hang him is no punishment. Didn't Christ tell the thieves on the Cross, *You shall be with me in Paradise today*? Why release him to the pleasure of Heaven before he has repaid his debts on Earth? He set my poor parents to work themselves away, to live in poverty, while they paid him to live in comfort. A far harsher punishment, I think, would be to make

48

him pay back all the money he tricked from them, with fifteen per cent interest – for if my parents had lent him the money, he would have to pay it back with interest.'

'That would be a fortune!' said the Chaplain, but then added, 'I will pay it, I will pay it willingly, Your Majesty; I'll sell everything I own, I promise!'

'Be silent, sir! What is your promise worth?' said the Queen. 'You have more to say, Thomas? Go on.'

'Only, Your Majesty,' said Thomas, 'that my old parents have no need of this money now they are under my roof. I shall see that they never want. And I will never allow people to say that I want this money for myself – so let this good man of God here use the money to build houses for poor old people who can no longer work and have nowhere to go. Let him give them three good meals every day, and good clothes and shoes. And appoint honest men to check how the money is spent, and to see that he plays no more of his jokes. In this way, Your Majesty, my old parents will never discover how they were fooled; but good will have come of the cruel trick in the end.'

'A good idea, Thomas,' said the Queen, 'but I'm loathe to leave his neck unbroken. I must consider. Guards! Take the Chaplain – the ex-Chaplain – into custody.' And the Queen left the room in a terrible temper.

6

The Chaplain's Punishment

The Chaplain spent the worst night of his life in a jail cell. His bed was hard, and he was cold, and the food was too disgusting to eat, even if he had had any appetite. He couldn't sleep for worrying about whether he was to make that dreadful walk through the streets to the scaffold where he would be hung. And yet he wasn't sorry for what he had done to the old couple; he was only sorry about what was being done to him.

But he remained there for five days while the Queen considered, and soon he began to feel very hungry, for the food provided by the jailer was little and bad. As his clothes grew damp in the damp cell, they let the cold through to his body, and he was frozen, and stiff in his joints. And he said to himself, 'If it hurts like this to be hungry; if you are cold like this when your clothes are few and old, then indeed, what I did to the old couple was wicked, and I deserve to be punished.'

But he still hoped the punishment wouldn't be hanging.

At the end of five days he was released and brought before the Queen; and there, too, was the hateful Master Thomas Katt, with his handsome ginger beard, and his fine clothes.

'Prisoner,' said the Queen to him, 'I still incline to break your neck, for I think, once it is broken, you will never commit a crime again; but Master Katt has persuaded me to let you live, on condition that you spend your life in working for the poor.'

'Thank you, Your Majesty, thank you, thank you!'

'Give no thanks to me,' said the Queen. 'I was for hanging you. Thank Master Thomas Katt.'

'Give no thanks to me,' said Thomas Katt. 'Instead, shake my hand, and come home to dinner with me. My parents will be delighted to see their old friend, who gave their kitten such an education!'

'Oh no – please, excuse me,' said the Chaplain. 'I couldn't bear . . .'

'I insist,' said Master Katt. 'We can tell them about our plans for the alms-houses.'

And the Chaplain was made to go back to Thomas Katt's house, where the old couple recognised him and greeted him with enthusiastic thanks. The Chaplain had a harder job to recognise them, for they were now dressed in beautiful clothes, and the thin, tired old faces he remembered had grown chubby and pink. Such a change had come over them that the Chaplain felt quite ashamed at the change *he* had once made to them. The old pair chattered at him all the time, asking him to admire what a fine man their kitten had grown to be, and congratulating him on the success of his teaching. They dragged him into every room of the house, to see what fine things Thomas had, and what fine things Thomas had bought them; and about everything they said, 'We shouldn't have it, if it weren't for you!'

The Chaplain was in an agony of embarrassment and guilt; and all the time he knew that Thomas Katt was laughing at him, though there was not even a smile on Thomas Katt's face.

Over dinner, Thomas explained to his parents that he and his old teacher were thinking of building houses for poor old people who had nowhere to go. The old couple thought it a wonderful idea.

'Thanks to you, Chaplain, our Thomas has done so well, and he looks after us,' said the old woman, 'but without Thomas, where should we be when we were too old to work our farm?'

'Thomas, how do we get hold of that money you've been putting away for us?' the old man asked his son. 'You know, that money from the rent of our farm?'

'Why do you want it, Father?' Thomas asked.

'Because I'm thinking,' said the old man, looking at his wife, 'that we should like to give you - some money to help build these houses – to show how thankful we are to you and all you've done for us.'

'You gave enough when you educated me,' Thomas said.

'Oh, but we must give some!' said the old lady, taking one of her husband's hands and one of her son's. 'We never spend it, Tommy, and you won't use it – so put it to some good use.'

'Very well,' Thomas said. 'Tell me how much you wish to give, and I'll see that it's paid.' And he smiled across the table at the Chaplain, who was shamed again and felt wretched.

And so it was that the Queen's Chaplain left his comfortable post in her household, sold every single thing he owned, and used all the money to build alms-houses for twenty poor old people. They were small houses, but the Queen herself would not have despised them, with their chimneys and warm hearths, with their glassed windows and benches outside, in gardens of gilly-flowers and lavender. And all the old people who moved into them were clothed warmly from head to foot, and given shoes for their feet; and every day food was brought to them, and fuel in the winter, so they had no fear of freezing or starving. And people said what a good man the Queen's Chaplain was – what a true Christian. But such a sad man, they said; he always looked so worried, and he hardly ever smiled.

They didn't know how much the Chaplain dreaded the visits of Mr. Thomas Katt, who came to see the old people in the alms-houses often, in his orange velvet suit and silk-lined cloak. He would talk with the old people for hours, asking them how they liked their houses, and their meals, and clothes; and how they liked the Chaplain. Was the Chaplain helpful? Did he deal with their complaints as they would wish? And the Chaplain would see them talking, and would feel quite ill with the dread that one of the old people might be saying something bad about him, which would annoy Master Katt.

But there was worse; for at the end of every visit Mr. Thomas Katt would come to the house where the Chaplain now lived, and ask to look at the account books, where the Chaplain had to write down every penny he received for the old people, and every penny he spent. And Master Katt would

check through it all, to make sure that the Chaplain was spending all the money on the old people, and no more on himself than he had to.

Master Katt was always polite and friendly, and always smiled as he handed the account book back to the Chaplain, but how the Chaplain hated him! And how afraid he was of Master Katt; and how miserable he always was, because he never knew when Master Katt might visit. He missed his old life, with its comfort, its wine and books and music, very much. But, whenever he was most filled with hate and anger, he would remember that it was all because he had cheated the old couple of *their* comforts, and he had no one to blame for that but himself. Truly, as Thomas Katt had said, it was a worse punishment than the whipping and hanging the Chaplain himself had suggested; for that would have been over in a single day. But the task of looking after the alms-houses went on and on, day after day, to his life's end.

As for the old couple, they lived with Thomas Katt, and believed him their son, until the end of their days; and, as he had promised, they never wanted for anything. True, they missed him when he was away at sea, but when he married, he left his wife in their care when he sailed, and the old couple positively swelled with pride, and doted on their new daughter, and on their granddaughter too, when she was born.

And Thomas, when he returned again, completed their pride and their joy, by building a grand new house on their land in the country, where they had once farmed. He took all his family on a journey to see the house being built, and was careful to ask the old couple's advice on everything, which made them feel wonderfully wise.

'To think,' said the old man, 'that a gentleman's house should stand where our old farmhouse did!'

'And that we should live in it!' said the old woman. 'Oh, old man, it was the best thing we ever did, having our Tommy educated!'

Over every doorway in the house Thomas Katt had carved the merchant's motto, *God give me good venture* and the head of a cat; for, he said, all his happiness came from his having been a cat. And when the old couple died, at the end of a happy old age, he had them buried in the local church. In their grave he laid with them the drawstring bag and the bones of their murdered kitten; and above their grave he set a statue of them sitting together, with a small cat lying between them. And his own tomb, when he died, had a carving of him lying asleep, with his hand resting on a sleeping cat. And written on his tomb are the words, *Here lies the Tom-Kitten that grew to be a Tom-Katt.*